AGE OF DINOSAURS: **VELOCIRAPTOR**

AGE OF DINOSAURS:

Velociraptor

SHERYL PETERSON

CREATIVE EDUCATION

Published by Creative Education
P.O. Box 227, Mankato, Minnesota 56002
Creative Education is an imprint of The Creative Company
www.thecreativecompany.us

Design and production by Blue Design
Art direction by Rita Marshall
Printed by Corporate Graphics in the United States of America

Photographs by Alamy (Patrik Ružic), Corbis (Mitchell Gerber, Louie Psihoyos, Louie Psihoyos/Science Faction), Getty Images (Max Dannenbaum, DEA Picture Library, Dorling Kindersley, Gary Ombler, Topical Press Agency, Yoshikazu Tsuno/AFP), iStockphoto (John Carnemolla, Jim Jurica, Angie Sharp), Library of Congress, Sarah Yakawonis/Blue Design

Library of Congress Cataloging-in-Publication Data
Peterson, Sheryl.
Velociraptor / by Sheryl Peterson.
p. cm. — (Age of dinosaurs)
Summary: An introduction to the life and era of the swift, carnivorous dinosaur known as *Velociraptor*, starting with the creature's 1923 discovery and ending with present-day research topics.
Includes bibliographical references and index.
ISBN 978-1-58341-979-3
1. Velociraptor—Juvenile literature. I. Title. II. Series.

QE862.S3.P486 2010
567.912—dc22   2009025540

CPSIA: 120109 PO1089

First Edition
9 8 7 6 5 4 3 2 1

CONTENTS

VELOCIRAPTOR TALES

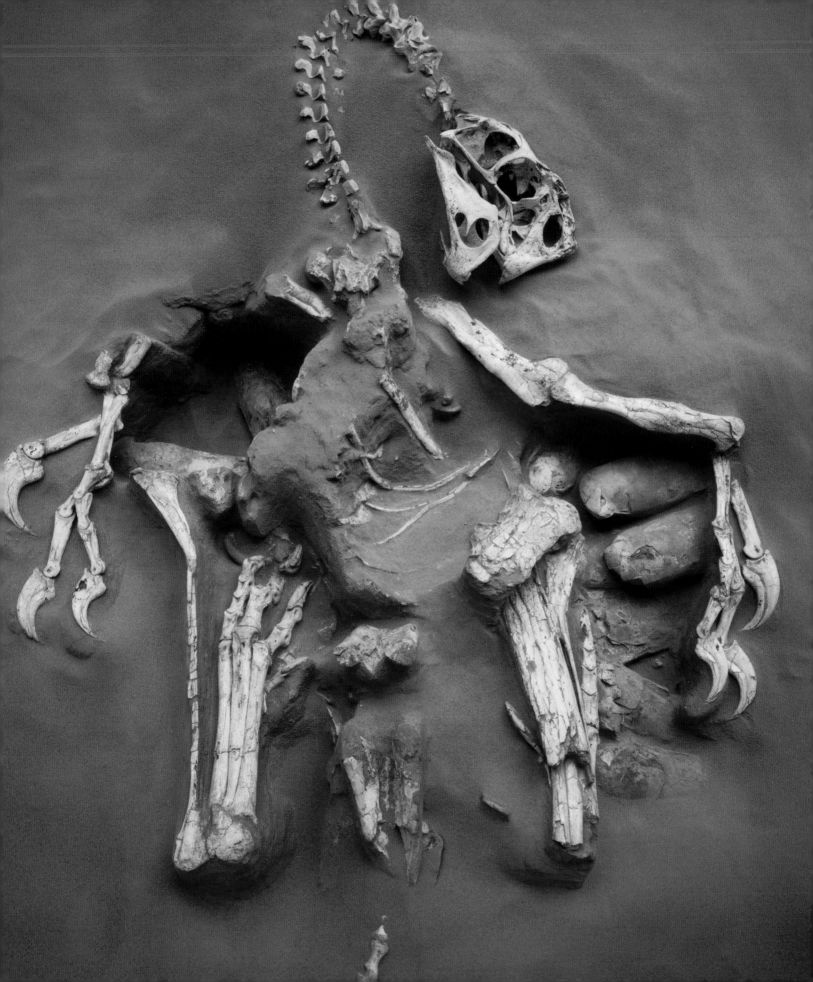

GOBI DESERT DISCOVERIES

With a wide-brimmed hat atop his head and a six-shooter strapped to his hip, Roy Chapman Andrews battled against blistering sandstorms, wild dogs, and even venomous snakes. Nothing could stop the explorer from his dinosaur fossil quest. The tent-dwellers who lived in the Gobi Desert of Mongolia were amused by Andrews and called him "The Dragon Hunter."

It was 1923, and some contemporaries thought Andrews's plan was crazy. The Gobi Desert was two-thirds the size of Texas, and the automobiles he was using to cross it were a relatively new, untested invention. But Andrews did not listen and led his parade of Dodge cars across the scorching Gobi sands. He was returning to an area of the desert known as the "Flaming Cliffs" with his scientific team from New York's American Museum of Natural History in search of ancient bones. Even though he was sometimes attacked by roving bandits, Andrews drove on through the far reaches of China, where a car had never been seen before. Spare tires and gasoline had to be carted in on the humped backs of camels. At times, the sore-footed camels were fitted with patches from used car tires to help cushion their steps.

On his first trip into the Gobi in 1922, Andrews and his team had found the remains of a new dinosaur, which was later named *Protoceratops*. If the parrot-beaked, frill-headed dinosaur had lived in the region of the orange-red cliffs, Andrews knew there were bound

The *Oviraptor* discovered in the Gobi Desert sands by Roy Chapman Andrews, and at first misidentified, likely died while protecting its eggs.

to be more animal remains nearby. The Gobi's sand and low **humidity** provided the perfect conditions for preserving fossils.

Andrews was proven correct when, in July 1923, the team uncovered an amazing find. On a sandstone ridge, they discovered a ring of brown, oblong dinosaur eggs with eggshell fragments all around. On top of the nest was a small dinosaur skeleton. Prior to the discovery, scientists could only theorize that dinosaurs laid eggs like other **reptiles**, and eggs that had been found earlier in England and France were dismissed as belonging to ancient birds. By the end of the expedition, Andrews and his coworkers had recovered 25 eggs in all. Andrews concluded that the mother dinosaur covered the eggs with a thin layer of sand and left them to be hatched by the sun's rays. (The fossil hunter assumed that the nest belonged to *Protoceratops*, but it was later determined to belong to a new birdlike dinosaur, *Oviraptor*.)

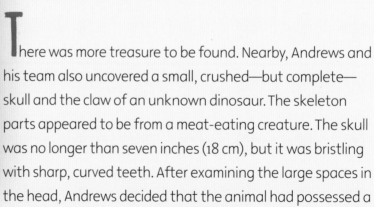

Roy Andrews made his first expedition for the American Museum in 1908—to Alaska—and served as the museum's director from 1935 to 1942.

There was more treasure to be found. Nearby, Andrews and his team also uncovered a small, crushed—but complete—skull and the claw of an unknown dinosaur. The skeleton parts appeared to be from a meat-eating creature. The skull was no longer than seven inches (18 cm), but it was bristling with sharp, curved teeth. After examining the large spaces in the head, Andrews decided that the animal had possessed a large brain and big, alert eyes. The claw of the second digit of the foot was flattened like it is on modern birds of prey such as falcons.

Back in the United States, Henry Fairfield Osborn, famed

Mistaken Egg Identity

In 1923, the American Museum of Natural History's expedition found the skull of a bizarre toothless dinosaur lying on top of a "nest" of bits of dinosaur eggs. Since *Protoceratops* was the most commonly found dinosaur in the area, paleontologist Henry Fairfield Osborn assumed that the eggs had belonged to *Protoceratops* and that the other dinosaur had been in the process of robbing the nest when its skull was crushed by a defensive *Protoceratops* mother. Osborn named the dinosaur *Oviraptor philoceratops*, the first part of the name meaning "egg seizer" and the second part signifying "lover of ceratopsians." However, about 70 years later, based on the results from studies of embryos discovered in Mongolia, scientists realized that Osborn had made a mistake. These new fossils were found to be related to *Oviraptor* and showed that the eggs probably belonged to the toothless theropod itself. It had been protecting its own eggs, not stealing another's. The birdlike dinosaur laid clutches of 15 to 20 eggs and arranged them in a circle in a nest. Then it appears to have sat on the eggs to keep them warm.

Paleontologist

H. F. Osborn

paleontologist and president of the American Museum of Natural History, congratulated Andrews on his discovery of a new dinosaur **species**. Osborn said, "You have written a new chapter in the history of life upon the earth." He named the new animal *Velociraptor mongoliensis*, designating it as having lived in Mongolia. *Velociraptor* meant "swift thief" and was aptly named, considering Osborn originally thought that *Velociraptor* stole other dinosaurs' eggs for food. Osborn believed that *Velociraptor* had lived approximately 75 million years ago during the Cretaceous Period.

However, the discovery of the dinosaur eggs eclipsed the lowly *Velociraptor* bones. The small dinosaur's skeleton did attract some interest because of certain birdlike features, but no one would know the real nature of the beast until many decades after the American Museum explorers had left the Gobi Desert.

After *Velociraptor* was discovered, paleontologists continued their careful efforts to dig up other kinds of raptors in the fossil-rich Gobi Desert.

During the **Cold War** years, North American teams were shut out of Mongolia by the Soviet Union. Meanwhile, expeditions led by Soviet, Polish, Chinese, and Canadian scientists went on to recover several more amazing *Velociraptor* specimens. In 1990, American scientists finally received permission to return to the Gobi Desert fossil fields. The paleontologists soon turned up more well-preserved *Velociraptor* fossils. One was jokingly nicknamed "Ichabodcraniosaurus" because a complete specimen was found without its skull. This was in reference to the character Ichabod Crane in Washington Irving's story "The Legend of Sleepy Hollow," in

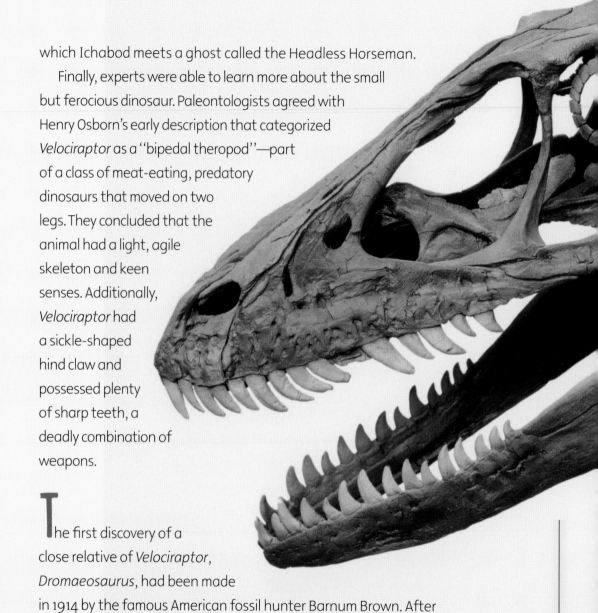

which Ichabod meets a ghost called the Headless Horseman.

　　Finally, experts were able to learn more about the small but ferocious dinosaur. Paleontologists agreed with Henry Osborn's early description that categorized *Velociraptor* as a "bipedal theropod"—part of a class of meat-eating, predatory dinosaurs that moved on two legs. They concluded that the animal had a light, agile skeleton and keen senses. Additionally, *Velociraptor* had a sickle-shaped hind claw and possessed plenty of sharp teeth, a deadly combination of weapons.

The first discovery of a close relative of *Velociraptor*, *Dromaeosaurus*, had been made in 1914 by the famous American fossil hunter Barnum Brown. After Andrews found the first *Velociraptor* fragments, scientists began to compare notes about bone structure and other similar details of the

DROMAEOSAURID

Velociraptor relative

Dromaeosaurid

two dinosaurs, but each remained classified as belonging to different dinosaur families for decades.

However, when Yale University paleontologist John Ostrom began studying the species *Deinonychus* in 1964, he discovered that it was another North American relative of *Velociraptor*. Five years later, Ostrom grouped *Velociraptor*, *Deinonychus*, and *Dromaeosaurus* in a new family called Dromaeosauridae.

Ostrom demonstrated that, aside from being deadly hunters, the dromaeosaurids shared certain skeletal features with primitive birds. He proposed that dinosaurs were more like large non-flying birds than they were akin to lizards. Scientists began to wonder if birds had **evolved** from dinosaurs. However, finding real proof of a connection proved to be a problem. There was no concrete evidence linking dinosaur and bird behavior.

Meaning "terrible claw," the Early Cretaceous raptor *Deinonychus* was named for the sickle-shaped claw it had on the second toe of each foot.

FAST AND FEROCIOUS

Like other dromaeosaurids, *Velociraptor* had a deadly claw on each foot, which it used to strike down prey and possibly fend off competitors.

Velociraptor was small but possessed deadly speed. The animal was probably no more than 6 feet (1.8 m) long from its snout to the tip of its tail, weighed about 33 pounds (15 kg), and stood only 3 to 4 feet (0.9–1.2 m) tall. That would have made it about the size of a large turkey. *Velociraptor*'s body was perfectly suited for its extremely active lifestyle of running over miles of hot sand dunes in its Gobi Desert home. It would have had to adjust to the scarcity of water, as well as to the colder temperatures that occurred at night.

As a dromaeosaurid, *Velociraptor* was a carnivore, or meat-eater. Its muscular jaws contained about 80 sharp, curved teeth. The animal's skull had two big eye sockets, which meant that it probably had large eyes and good vision. Because of where the sockets are placed, experts know that *Velociraptor*'s eyes did not face forward as those of *Tyrannosaurus rex* and other hunters did. Its eyes looked out from the side of its head, like a bird's, giving it a wide-angle view. Many scientists believe that *Velociraptor* hunted at night, relying on its **binocular** vision and keen sense of smell.

A multitude of bones and long strings of tendons in *Velociraptor*'s tail kept it stiff and straight. The tail worked as a counterbalance that allowed the animal to make quick turns while running. Like birds, *Velociraptor* also had a unique wrist joint that enabled the dinosaur to fold its arms like wings and had bones that were full of air pockets.

Even the dinosaur's feet were like many modern birds', with four toes on each foot. Many scientists think that *Velociraptor* was covered with fuzz or feathers, too. Feathers would have helped shield its skin from the sun's rays and kept the dinosaur warm at night. The presence of feathers does not indicate that it flew, though.

Velociraptor could sustain a running speed of about 25 miles (40 km) per hour, comparable to today's ostriches. It might also have been able to attain speeds of 40 miles (64 km) per hour for short bursts, and most scientists agree that the fleet-footed *Velociraptor* could jump. The little speedster ran on its two muscular legs, leaving its long arms free. Not many plant-eaters would have been able to outrun an attacking *Velociraptor*, since its highly efficient respiratory system allowed it to breathe easily at any speed. Also, by using its strong sense of smell, the dinosaur would have been able to smell an injured or dying animal and seek it out for an easy meal.

Velociraptor had a flat nose and an unusually large head relative to its body size. The head likely contained a sizable brain, indicating that *Velociraptor* was quite smart for a dinosaur. As measured by the ratio of its brain to body mass, the creature possessed a high level of intelligence and was about as smart as present-day large cats such as lions. Scientists think that the cunning *Velociraptor* most likely used its large brain to hunt cooperatively to achieve the best results when tracking down plant-eaters of lesser intelligence.

Pound for pound, *Velociraptors* were powerful predators and spent their days constantly on the move. They had a rare combination of foot,

Although it could run like an ostrich (below), a lone *Velociraptor* could have faced a fight when encountering its common prey, *Protoceratops*.

hand, and head weaponry. Fierce claws were the *Velociraptor*'s deadliest weapon. Even though the *Velociraptor* walked only on its third and fourth toes, every finger and toe had a claw. The first toe ended in a small **dewclaw**, but the second toe of each foot had a curved claw up to four inches (10 cm) long. When *Velociraptor* tensed its toe muscles, the claws swung down with frightening force that could penetrate and snag.

It would have been difficult for larger plant-eating dinosaurs such as duck-billed hadrosaurs to escape from a *Velociraptor* pack. The small but quick dinosaurs had long arms with powerful, clawed hands. These claws could grab, slash, and kill a victim in no time. *Velociraptors* attacked slower-moving animals of various sizes by jumping at the animal with claws outstretched and then repeatedly dragging the sharpest claw down the skin, inflicting fatal wounds. Their jagged teeth would have finished off the unlucky victim.

A typical prey animal for *Velociraptor* was *Protoceratops*. This **herbivore** would have roamed the desert in herds, snuffling and snorting like pigs, looking for vegetation. Occasionally, dust may have flown when a pair of *Protoceratops* began butting heads over a prime food source or competition for a mate. If a pack of *Velociraptors* were nearby, the predators would have stopped racing across the sand dunes and watched the battle from afar. Taut and erect, they would have perched on thin, muscular hind limbs, their forelegs off the ground. Their dragon-like heads would have remained still, while their piercing eyes took in every movement.

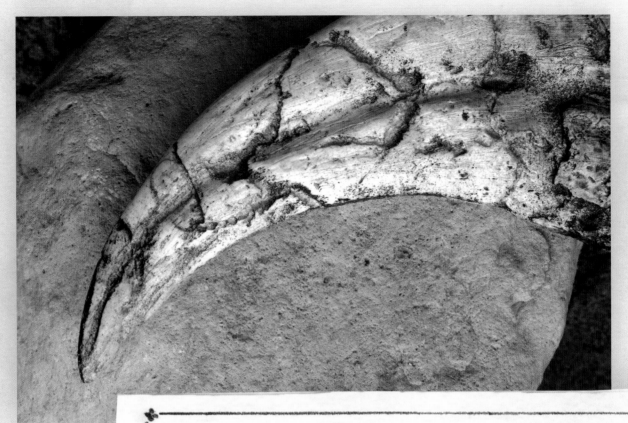

Terminator Toe

No animal wanted to be kicked by *Velociraptor*. Its hind legs were long and powerful, with a pronounced knob at the top of the upper leg bone. This knob was probably where a strong tendon attached to bone to enable the animal's leg-kicking action. But the deadliest part of the dinosaur was its feet. *Velociraptor*'s feet had four toes, but the second toe was "the terminator." The second toe's claw was enormous and shaped like a half-moon, or sickle, which ended in a nasty hook. The individual bones on this second digit were specially designed for flexibility. When *Velociraptor* was running, the toe was retracted upward so it would not slow the dinosaur's speed. Retraction also prevented the claw from getting dull, because it never touched the ground. The claw had only one purpose—to stab prey. After *Velociraptor* grabbed a small **mammal** or an unsuspecting *Protoceratops* with its strong arms, the second claw would snap up with great speed and savage force. Scientists believe that *Velociraptor* used its killer claws to bring down an animal before it ever used its teeth.

The Real Indiana Jones

Explorer Roy Chapman Andrews always said he was "born under a lucky star," since he survived so many narrow escapes from danger. Andrews had a love of adventure that took him all around the globe. His engaging personality and thorough planning helped him obtain funds from wealthy philanthropists such as J. P. Morgan and John D. Rockefeller. Andrews led five scientific expeditions to Mongolia's Gobi Desert between 1922 and 1930. He was a pioneer in modern field research, but it was his fossil discoveries that stunned the world and catapulted him to fame, as he found the first *Velociraptor* and *Protoceratops* skeletons and the first nest of preserved dinosaur eggs. These findings were remarkable for a man who began his scientific career by scrubbing the floors at the American Museum of Natural History in New York City. Twenty-one years after his death, Hollywood created a character based on Andrews' life. The archaeologist Indiana Jones, played by actor Harrison Ford, was the hero of three enormously popular action movies of the 1980s. Yet Andrews' real-life adventures were even more exciting because they were true.

The *Velociraptor* pack might then have exploded into action. They would have swished across the sand in a pack of four or five and cut a blurring swath through the *Protoceratops* herd, much like a pack of wolves taking down a caribou or deer. The slower creatures would have had little chance to react, and several of the stocky dinosaurs would have been held tightly and clawed to death. The unharmed *Protoceratops* would have stampeded into the dunes, leaving the vicious *Velociraptors* to devour the remaining feast.

But *Velociraptor* didn't always dine on large dinosaurs; it also preyed on smaller creatures such as lizards and insects, while juveniles lived by raiding the eggs and hatchlings of other dinosaurs. *Velociraptor*'s digestive system was incapable of processing plant fibers.

Although no *Velociraptor* eggs have been discovered, there is evidence that leads many paleontologists to believe that the creatures laid their eggs in nests and sat on them until they hatched. Roy Chapman Andrews's 1923 discovery of *Oviraptor* eggs proved that dinosaurs laid their eggs in clusters, sometimes in a circle, in a nest they dug out and covered over with leaves or sand. Most likely, *Velociraptor*'s eggs would have been no larger than a tennis ball. Like birds, the dinosaurs would have laid 10 to 15 eggs only once a year. The babies would have grown fast after hatching and doubled their size in just six weeks.

Even while studying the eggs of an *Oviraptor* (above), Andrews looked the part of a 1920s adventurer accustomed to working in the field.

25

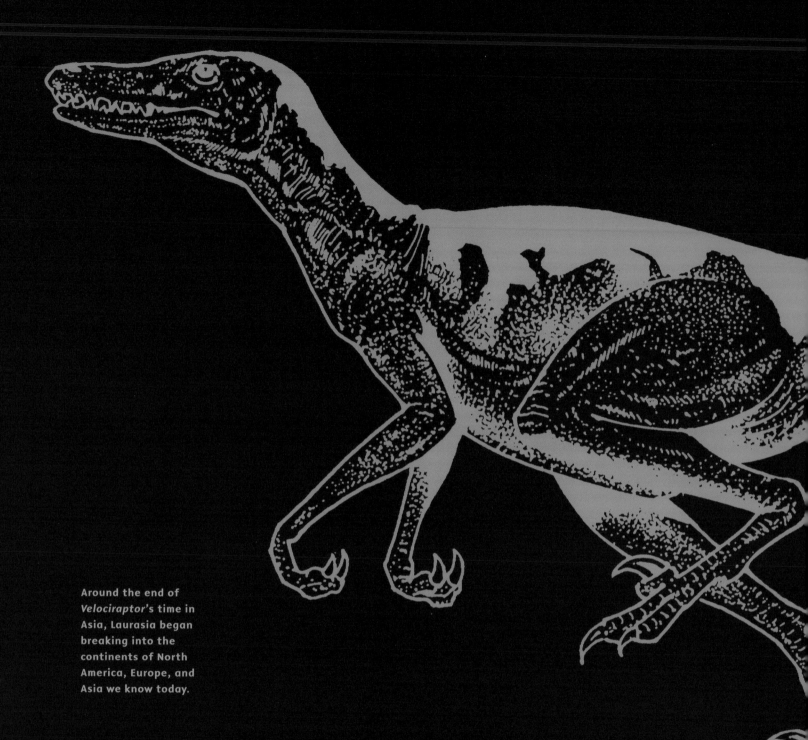

Around the end of *Velociraptor*'s time in Asia, Laurasia began breaking into the continents of North America, Europe, and Asia we know today.

CRETACEOUS DESERT HOME

When *Velociraptor* was alive during the Cretaceous Period, the earth was a warm place—so warm, in fact, that the North and South poles had no ice. The damp **climate** that had developed by the end of the Jurassic (144 million years ago) extended into the Cretaceous, enabling the dinosaurs and other reptiles to keep evolving into new forms as older ones became **extinct**. Climates became more seasonal, with winter and summer and wet and dry times. Greater extremes developed between temperatures at the poles and those near the equator.

The continents, which scientists believe had once been a giant supercontinent called Pangaea during the mid-Triassic Period, continued to pull away from one another, creating new seas and oceans. North America and South America drifted farther apart from Europe and Africa, and the Atlantic Ocean was formed. Many mountain ranges developed during this period, including the Rocky Mountains in North America and the European Alps.

Since land animals could no longer walk freely around the globe, and plant life could not be spread as easily, species unique to each continent began to develop. Ants crawled, butterflies and dragonflies flitted from blossom to blossom, and small mammals scurried through wooded areas. Wild dogs called dholes became common in Asia. Giant marine lizards called mosasaurs developed paddle-like limbs and jaws resembling those of modern crocodiles.

Many other life forms began appearing in the Cretaceous. Abundant rain helped flowering plants, such as the magnolia, to appear and soon dominate the land. The variety of flowers encouraged the evolution of new forms of insects. Forests of broad-leaved trees such as oaks and beeches began to flourish and replace many of the **conifers** and ferns of the earlier period. These conditions provided new food sources for browsing dinosaurs, but they also gave ample cover to their predators. Dinosaurs getting a drink at a river could be surprised easily by a predator hiding in a forest along the riverbank.

Plant-eating *Saurolophus* fell prey to pack hunters such as *Velociraptor*, their 30- to 40-foot (9–12 m) bodies providing ample food for the meat-eaters.

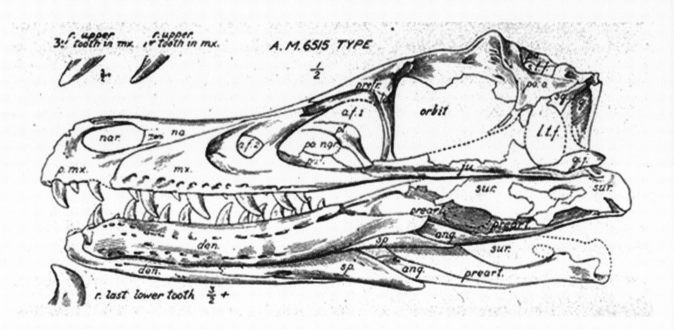

During this era, flying reptiles called pterosaurs—such as *Ornithocheirus*, *Pteranodon*, and *Quetzalcoatlus*—were able to glide long distances, possibly even across continents. *Quetzalcoatlus*, a spectacular creature with a 40-foot (12 m) wingspan, is thought to have been the largest flying animal ever. Meanwhile, birds developed into two types: flying and flightless. Some of the earliest fossils from the Cretaceous resemble modern loons, cormorants, pelicans, flamingos, and sandpipers.

Velociraptor's home, the Gobi Desert of central Asia, stretched for 1,000 miles (1,609 km) across what is now southeast Mongolia and northern China. Then, as today, it would have been a dry, sandy, inhospitable landscape, where temperatures dropped below freezing at night, then became baking hot in the daytime sun. In the Gobi, there were only a few streams available for marine life. Sharing *Velociraptor*'s desert habitat were both skinny lizards with long tails

The Flaming Cliffs

One of the world's largest dinosaur graveyards is in an area of the Gobi Desert known as the Flaming Cliffs. Nicknamed by Roy Chapman Andrews, the cliffs in this region are made of orange-red sandstone and, at sunset, seem to glow as if they are on fire. Temperatures in this vast and inhospitable place drop well below freezing at night and then become scorching hot with the daytime sun. The six-mile (9.7 km) stretch of dry, rocky terrain has yielded incredibly well-preserved dinosaur fossils of the Late Cretaceous Period. Many of the fossils appear to have been buried by sudden swirling sandstorms that blew over and entombed the animals. A large number of *Protoceratops* skeletons have been found standing in an upright position, as if frozen in time. Today, camels, golden eagles, and gazelles inhabit the area, along with rare animals such as the Gobi bear. The Flaming Cliffs has become a tourist attraction where visitors can search for dinosaur eggshells in the dunes. Paleontologists also continue to mine the sandy site for fossilized bones, dinosaur eggs, and nests.

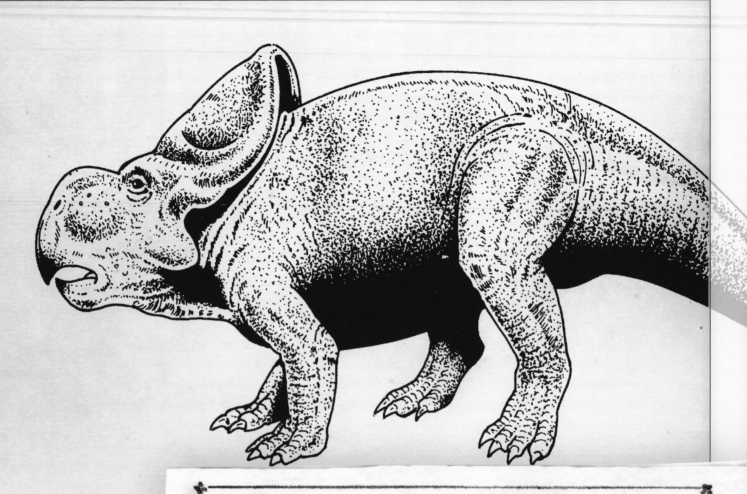

Bountiful meal

Protoceratops

Velociraptor's Favorite Meal

A small, sturdy dinosaur was often dinner for *Velociraptor*. *Protoceratops* (whose name means "first horned face"), was a ceratopsian, which means it was related to other horned herbivores such as *Torosaurus* and *Triceratops*. Since *Protoceratops* was an abundant species and not as large as later ceratopsians, it was near the bottom of the desert **food chain**. So common was *Protoceratops* in the Mongolia of 75 million years ago that it has been nicknamed the "Sheep of the Cretaceous." *Protoceratops* had a stout, barrel-shaped body that provided some protection from the desert sun, a beaked snout, and a large neck frill. The frill grew as the dinosaur aged but had two large holes that were covered with skin, helping to reduce the frill's weight. As an herbivore, *Protoceratops* wandered the barren landscape in herds, searching for fresh leaves. Most of the time, though, *Protoceratops* found food by digging up buried roots or tubers and using its sharp beak to slice through the tough plant skin. Dozens of complete *Protoceratops* skeletons have been recovered from deserts in Mongolia and China.

and massive, wrinkled lizards. *Velociraptor* was the showpiece of the desert, though. It was fast, smart, and the ultimate predatory machine. Apart from the stout *Protoceratops*, there were also the small, toothless *Oviraptor*, the ostrich-like *Gallimimus*, and the duck-billed *Saurolophus* wandering in the desert for *Velociraptor* to stalk.

Fortunately for *Velociraptor,* it lived before its later-Cretaceous North American cousin *Deinonychus*. This species was bigger (weighing about 175 pounds, or 80 kg), had longer claws on each of its fingers and toes, and likely could have taken down a *Velociraptor* if the two had lived in the same place at the same time. However, the smaller dinosaur enjoyed its place at the top of the desert food chain most of the time.

Velociraptor skeletons have been found in the Asian regions of Mongolia, Russia, and China, but a total of only 12 specimens have been dug up. That has not given scientists much to study, and no one knows why *Velociraptor* suddenly became extinct about 70 million years ago. Scientists now believe that the world started to get cooler around that time, though, and *Velociraptor* may not have been able to adapt and keep itself warm. Even bedding down under a cover of leaves and branches may not have been enough.

Saurolophus belonged to the most common family of dinosaurs, the hadrosaurs, which were characterized mainly by toothless, duck-billed beaks.

33

About five million years later, all of the flying reptiles and dinosaurs gradually disappeared during a mass extinction at the end of the Cretaceous. Some scientists believe that around 85 percent of other animal species alive at the time were also wiped out. The cause of the mass extinction, known as the K-T (Cretaceous-Tertiary) extinction event, is still a matter of debate, but one possible explanation involves an increased amount of volcanic activity at that time. The volcanic eruptions could have trapped heat radiating from the earth, raising temperatures and drying significant portions of land, or they could have also thrown so much dust into the air that the sun was blotted out. Most scientists think that a huge meteor struck the earth and interfered with plants' growth around that same time, reducing the amount of sunlight and causing widespread disruptions in global food chains. Following that disastrous event would have been several months of global darkness and freezing weather. With their food source severely depleted, the herbivores would have grown weaker and been eaten by carnivores. Eventually, all the dinosaurs would have perished.

Although exactly what happened may never be known, 65 million years ago, all of the dinosaurs, flying pterosaurs, and marine reptiles went the way of *Velociraptor*. The smaller animals that survived to see the Tertiary Period were the ancestors of today's animal species.

Meteor Impact Theory

In 1978, a huge impact crater dating from 65 million years ago was discovered near the town of Chicxulub on the coast of the Yucatán Peninsula in Mexico. Since the crater is 110 miles (177 km) across, experts think it was made by a meteor big enough to have caused a global catastrophe. The crater size indicates that it was formed by a meteor about six miles (9.7 km) wide that struck Earth at a speed of about 62,000 miles (99,779 km) per hour. The impact would have caused a gigantic explosion that vaporized the meteor itself and hurled hot gases and debris into the atmosphere. The plume of debris would have risen into space and gradually enveloped the entire world. That would have spelled the end of most life on Earth. Smaller species of animals may have survived, but the giant dinosaurs would have perished. The Meteor Impact Theory was first suggested in 1980 by physicist Luis Alvarez and his son Walter, a geologist. They discovered the 65-million-year-old layer of iridium, a silvery-white metal, throughout Earth's soil that indicated a meteor had struck at that time.

FEATHERS AND FLIERS

Scientists used to think that dinosaurs dragged their tails on the ground like modern reptiles such as alligators and crocodiles. The fossils of such dinosaurs as *Velociraptor* tell a different story, though, showing only two sets of footprints and no line of tail-dragging in between. This suggests that dinosaurs could have run more quickly than present-day reptiles with their tails off the ground. The tail was likely used in a similar manner to a rudder on a boat to help *Velociraptor* turn quickly without losing speed or balance.

Likewise, many birds' tails perform a balancing function, and the common physical feature is one of many that have led scientists to theorize that birds and dinosaurs are related. Paleontologist John Ostrom's studies of *Deinonychus* and *Velociraptor* led to a new way of thinking about dinosaurs. Since *Velociraptor* was one of the most birdlike theropods, it is highly probable that its ancestors may have been fliers. Ostrom first suggested that the dromaeosaurids and birds evolved from a common Jurassic ancestor due to several shared physical features. Ostrom also thought that the small carnivore could have been **warm-blooded**, like birds, as this would have given it more energy with which to hunt and sustain its lifestyle. Since the beginning of the 20th century, the popular conception of dinosaurs had been one of plodding, cold-blooded reptilian giants. Ostrom concluded that at least some dinosaurs had a high energy level and thus would have

A zoo in the central European city of Bratislava, Slovakia, features an exhibition of computer-controlled, life-size models of dinosaurs such as *Velociraptor*.

been at least partially warm-blooded. Thanks to Ostrom's and others' research, scientists once again became intrigued by dinosaurs in the late 1960s.

During the 1970s, dinosaur replicas and restorations were posed less like lizards and more like mammals and birds as a result of the new research. Nature artists such as Gregory S. Paul worked closely with paleontologists at various museums and institutions. They drew dinosaurs in more active poses and helped pioneer the renovated image of dinosaurs.

Depictions of *Velociraptor* have varied over the years, with scientists theorizing whether it had reptile-like skin or feathers and hair.

In 2007, paleontologists from the American Museum of Natural History and Chicago's Field Museum took a new look at some old bones. Scientists had long suspected that *Velociraptor* had had feathers, but they had not yet found any evidence that could confirm or disprove that theory. Then the team of Alan Turner, Peter Makovicky, and Mark Norell examined a well-preserved fossil of a *Velociraptor* forearm that had been unearthed in 1998 and found something of major importance. The men discovered raised areas of bone called quill knobs, evidence of where strong connective tissues called ligaments had attached flight feathers to bone. The scientists knew that quill knobs are found in every living bird species and are most evident in birds that are strong fliers. However, they continued to doubt that *Velociraptor* could have flown.

Since *Velociraptor* had short forelimbs compared to modern birds' wings, this has led some researchers to conclude that it was flightless

39

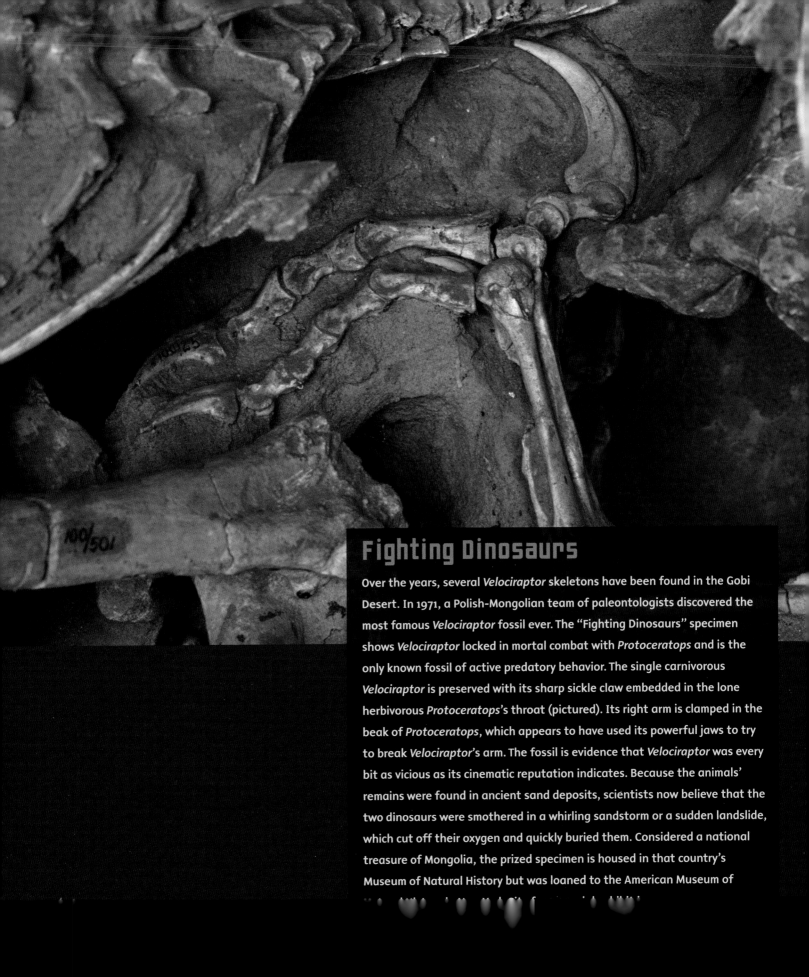

Fighting Dinosaurs

Over the years, several *Velociraptor* skeletons have been found in the Gobi Desert. In 1971, a Polish-Mongolian team of paleontologists discovered the most famous *Velociraptor* fossil ever. The "Fighting Dinosaurs" specimen shows *Velociraptor* locked in mortal combat with *Protoceratops* and is the only known fossil of active predatory behavior. The single carnivorous *Velociraptor* is preserved with its sharp sickle claw embedded in the lone herbivorous *Protoceratops*'s throat (pictured). Its right arm is clamped in the beak of *Protoceratops*, which appears to have used its powerful jaws to try to break *Velociraptor*'s arm. The fossil is evidence that *Velociraptor* was every bit as vicious as its cinematic reputation indicates. Because the animals' remains were found in ancient sand deposits, scientists now believe that the two dinosaurs were smothered in a whirling sandstorm or a sudden landslide, which cut off their oxygen and quickly buried them. Considered a national treasure of Mongolia, the prized specimen is housed in that country's Museum of Natural History but was loaned to the American Museum of but probably descended from an extinct creature that had been able to fly. That *Velociraptor* retained at least some feathers suggests that the covering continued to be used in some capacity, possibly for purposes of display, warmth, nest protection, or some other non-flight activity. *Velociraptor*'s large size was also likely a deterrent to flight.

Ancestors of *Velociraptor* may have lost their ability to fly but retained their feathers nonetheless. Mark Norell, **curator** of the American Museum of Natural History's paleontology division, summed up the findings by saying, "The more we learn about these animals, the more we find that there is basically no difference between birds and their closely related dinosaur ancestors like *Velociraptor*." He suggested that if *Velociraptor* were alive today, it would simply look like a very unusual bird.

Some scientists think that *Velociraptor* could have also used the feathers on its forelimbs for stability or lift when running or leaping. As examples, researchers point to the nearly perfect fossil specimens of small but advanced theropods found in China's Liaoning province in the 1990s. These newly discovered species all appear to have had a layering of feathers on their bodies in addition to feathers on their limbs that resembled wings. The turkey-sized *Caudipteryx* sported a plume of tail feathers, and its body showed an interesting mix of reptilian and birdlike features. Another small species, the crow-sized *Microraptor*, may have even been able to scale trees and glide through the air.

Caudipteryx, whose fossils date its existence to around 125 million years ago, had feathers covering most of its body but was unable to fly.

A life-size robotic *Velociraptor,* complete with a hairy mane and intimidating teeth, was displayed at an exhibit in Tokyo, Japan, in 2008.

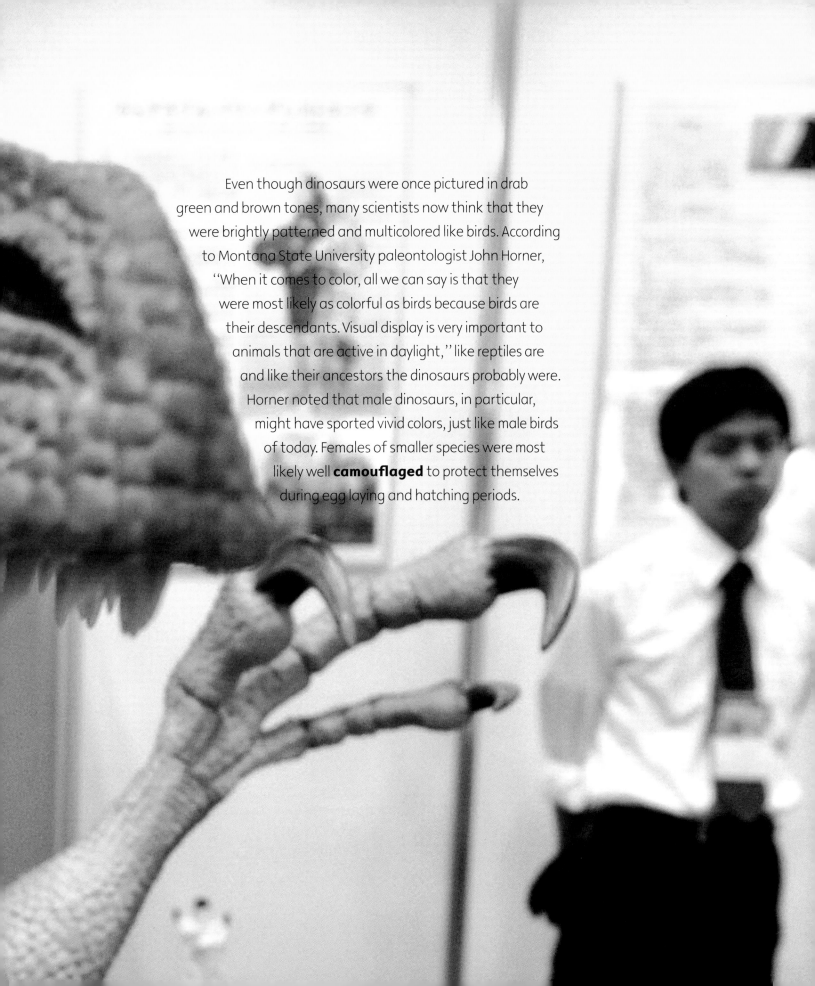

Even though dinosaurs were once pictured in drab
green and brown tones, many scientists now think that they
were brightly patterned and multicolored like birds. According
to Montana State University paleontologist John Horner,
''When it comes to color, all we can say is that they
were most likely as colorful as birds because birds are
their descendants. Visual display is very important to
animals that are active in daylight,'' like reptiles are
and like their ancestors the dinosaurs probably were.
Horner noted that male dinosaurs, in particular,
might have sported vivid colors, just like male birds
of today. Females of smaller species were most
likely well **camouflaged** to protect themselves
during egg laying and hatching periods.

Jurassic Park

In 1993, Steven Spielberg directed the hit movie *Jurassic Park*, which was based on a novel by Michael Crichton. In the movie, *Velociraptors* are depicted as sneaky, vicious creatures that attack people. They are also shown to be covered in scales, not fuzz or feathers, and are 400 percent larger than they were in real life. While the movie was being filmed in 1991, a new dinosaur named *Utahraptor* was discovered. Scientists decided it was a larger relative of *Velociraptor*. So perhaps the "raptors" in the *Jurassic Park* movie did exist—they just had the wrong name. But other movie details did not measure up, either. The Jurassic Period lasted from 208 to 144 million years ago. Neither *Utahraptor* nor *Velociraptor* lived during that time. They appeared millions of years later during the Cretaceous. Additionally, two of the movie's most vicious predators, *Tyrannosaurus rex* and *Velociraptor*, never even lived on the same continent in real life. *Jurassic Park* sequels came out in 1997 and 2001, and in all three films, *Velociraptor* could open doors and communicate with other "raptors."

For decades, *Velociraptor* was a dinosaur known only to scientists. Then, in 1993, the animal became famous with its starring role in the blockbuster movie *Jurassic Park*. However, the *Velociraptors* in the film were made to be far bigger and more intelligent than they would have been in real life. They were depicted as **genetically** revived creatures that were diabolically clever and ferocious predators, fond of hunting humans.

Even though *Velociraptor* lived about 80 million years ago, scientists have known about and studied the species for only about 85 years, looking for clues into the evolutionary history of modern birds. Since the days of explorers such as Roy Chapman Andrews, paleontology has become a more exact science. When *Velociraptor* specimens are found today, the first job is to record any valuable details, and then the fossil is carefully removed and made into a replica for a museum.

From collections of long-buried bones, scientists can reconstruct full skeletons and lifelike models of dinosaurs and other prehistoric creatures.

Every time a new fossil is found, scientists come closer to understanding what life on Earth was like millions of years ago. More than eight decades after the first *Velociraptor* fossils were discovered, scientists are still learning more about them and their reptilian relatives. And a century from now, they will probably have still more to discover.

Velociraptor compared with a five-foot-tall (152 cm) human

46

GLOSSARY

atmosphere—the layer of gases that surrounds Earth

binocular—using two eyes; also, the vision of two eyes

camouflaged—hidden, due to coloring or markings that blend in with a given environment

climate—the long-term weather conditions of an area

clutches—groups of eggs produced and incubated at the same time

Cold War—a period of intense political hostility between the United States and the Soviet Union that lasted from 1945 to 1990

conifers—evergreen trees, such as pines and firs, that bear cones

curator—the person in charge of a museum or art collection

dewclaw—a functionless inner toe of an animal that does not touch the ground

embryos—organisms in the early stages of development before they emerge from the egg

evolved—adapted or changed over time to survive in a certain environment

extinct—having no living members

food chain—a system in nature in which living things are dependent on each other for food

genetically—relating to genes, the basic physical units of heredity

herbivore—an animal that feeds only on plants

humidity—a quantity representing how much water vapor is present in the atmosphere

mammal—a warm-blooded animal that has a backbone and hair or fur, gives birth to live young, and produces milk to feed its young

paleontologist—a scientist who studies fossilized plants and animals

reptiles—cold-blooded animals with scaly skin that typically lay eggs on land

species—a group of living organisms that share similar characteristics and can mate with each other

warm-blooded—describing animals that maintain a constant body temperature, usually above the temperature of their surroundings

SELECTED BIBLIOGRAPHY

Farlow, James, and M. K. Brett-Surman. *The Complete Dinosaur.* Bloomington, Ind.: Indiana University Press, 1999.

Fastovsky, David. *The Evolution and Extinction of the Dinosaurs.* Cambridge: Cambridge University Press, 2005.

Haines, Tim, and Paul Chambers. *The Complete Guide to Prehistoric Life.* Buffalo, N.Y.: Firefly Books, 2007.

Malam, John, and John Woodward. *Dinosaur Atlas.* New York: DK Publishing, 2006.

Novacek, Michael. *Dinosaurs of the Flaming Cliffs.* Garden City, N.J.: Anchor Books, 1996.

Paul, Gregory. *Predatory Dinosaurs of the World.* New York: Simon and Schuster, 1988.

INDEX

READ MORE

Andrews, Roy. *Under a Lucky Star.*
  Madison, Wisc.: Borderland Books,
  2008.

Barrett, Paul. *National Geographic
  Dinosaurs.* Washington, D.C.:
  National Geographic Society, 2001.

Bausum, Ann. *Dragon Bones and
  Dinosaur Eggs: A Photobiography
  of Explorer Roy Chapman Andrews.*
  Washington D.C.: National
  Geographic Society, 2000.

Lambert, David. *The Ultimate
  Dinosaur Book.* New York: DK
  Publishing, 1993.

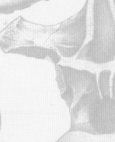